The Body Language Trail
Get Into The Mind

Jude D'Souza

Ukiyoto Publishing

All global publishing rights are held by

Ukiyoto Publishing

Published in 2023

Content Copyright © Jude D'Souza

ISBN 9789359208220

All rights reserved.
No part of this publication may be reproduced, transmitted, or stored in a retrieval system, in any form by any means, electronic, mechanical, photocopying, recording or otherwise, without the prior permission of the publisher.

The moral rights of the author have been asserted.

This book is sold subject to the condition that it shall not by way of trade or otherwise, be lent, resold, hired out or otherwise circulated, without the publisher's prior consent, in any form of binding or cover other than that in which it is published.

www.ukiyoto.com

Dedication

This book is dedicated to my heavenly virgin mother for making me excel in my career all through these years. She worked zealously and tirelessly to bring about such books as these to the readers. It is because of her that I am a good author, writer and more. All credit goes to her.

Acknowledgement

All thanks to the people whom I met in life for enriching my knowledge base about the nonverbal cues mentioned in this book. Every bit of it was God-ordained and all of them are precious in my life. I am on talking terms with every one of these precious people who have brought about such intellectual nourishment in my life and continue to do it so even today. God bless you.

Contents

Introduction	1
Scope Of This Book	2
Handshake	4
Sniffle	9
Playing With The Feet	15
The Perfectionist Touch	19
The Horizon Search	21
Anger-Exhibiting Cue	25
Fear-Exhibiting Cue	27
The Smartness-Exhibiting Cue	30
Callousness-Exhibiting Cue	32
Anxiety Exhibiting Cue	34
Epilogue	35
About the Author	*37*

Introduction

Human beings are quite complex to understand. One can know them by being close for quite a number of years as we know our best friends or family or acquaintances. But it is possible to get to know people through other means very quickly if close attention is paid to their body language and mannerisms. These are often truthful signs about what is going on in a person's mind, which don't tell lies.

Such truthful signs are used by psychiatrists and psychologists to evaluate people or treat them. Also, some investigative agencies or law enforcers tend to look for these to assess a suspect and even judges can look for them in witnesses to arrive at a judgment. But the judgment depends on the evidence brought forth and not this assessment.

This could be used by salespersons too to sell their products to prospects. But the assessment requires quite an amount of skill and some mavericks in this profession can easily find their way to the top of the corporate ladder by being well-versed with it.

The possibilities are limitless and one can only imagine the range of applications. I have listed quite a few of the important ones and each chapter is dedicated to each of the cues that can gauge a person's mindset or what is going on in his mind.

I learnt all of these through observing people for a few years and acquired these skills one by one. Experience is the best teacher as they say. And intellectuals have this skill in them innately learning without making an effort to dig deep into through books or other learning resources.

Also, as I found out that there is a dearth of these body language books looking into many nonverbal cues familiar to me from my own experience, I thought why not disseminate some knowledge from my own written work. Knowledge should be shared and as it is a gift, it should be made available to everyone in their bookshelf.

Scope of This Book

An old adage goes like this, 'Face is the index of mind'. True to this proverb, the face exhibits all that is inside the mind of an individual. It can range from a simple thing as a smile to much more complex ones that reveal the persona. The best part is that these things can never be hidden or manipulated by the person concerned and is revealed in plain sight to a good observer.

While speaking about nonverbal cues or body language in a person, the sum total is the information it conveys through conscious or subconscious body movements, facial expressions and gestures.

The area of study these aspects are covered in is called *kinesics*. It is a term coined by the American anthropologist Ray Birdwhistell.

Psychiatrists deal with such kind of nonverbal cues all the time. They seek these in their day-to-day patients to thoroughly gauge them and have a long checklist to measure their soundness of mind. They rely more heavily on facial gestures like the narrowing or state of eyes; position of mouth on the face; the frown on it and more. These can reveal emotions and more deeper insights into a person's mind.

Telling lies; anger; fear; shyness; extroversion; innocence; intellectual abilities and a lot of more can be revealed through these facial gestures. These professionals have a whole lot of tricks in their arsenal to have an insightful look into a person. They purportedly ask some questions to extract a response through nonverbal cues.

This book is not a work to get deep in to these complex nonverbal cues as facial gestures. These can get quite complex and require a good amount of experience to master and gain insight into a person's mind or intention.

More importantly, this work is to aid the common man with easily understandable and relatable nonverbal cues so that he can stay abreast—one step ahead—of the challenges posed in the harsh world outside.

To sum it up, this is also not a dainty stuff that belongs in the showcase, but practical information to use. As I have used it in my own life, here, I draw instances too from it so that it can be beneficial to the otherwise vulnerable ordinary person when faced with the demons of life.

References

www.thehansindia.com/hans/young-hans/face-is-the-index-of-mind--525232

Handshake

This kind of non-verbal cue is the most obvious form of getting to know the mind of the person and everyone is familiar with it. Greeting a person with a handshake is the common norm. It can tell a lot about the person to the one who is willing to observe.

Cold hands

For instance, if a person has cold hands and you feel it while shaking hands with him, it can mean he is nervous. My dad was called to a seminar at the bishop's house in my native to give a talk about the ongoing activities in his parish. This was done because he was teaching Catechism to students of many different grades in the elementary school, high school and also pre-university students of his concerned parish.

This opportunity was golden as he was selected from quite a good number of parishes in and around our area.

He was about to go to the dais to deliver a talk and he saw a familiar face in the crowd—a nun who was present—and she greeted him without him knowing her for quite a time. He extended his hand toward her for a handshake. She replied similarly too and pointed out to him that his hand is cold.

She could not understand what was going on in his mind. But my dad revealed to me after this incident—when he came home—that he was nervous because he was about to talk in front of a large number of consecrated people who have a God-ordained authority over our souls. This is quite expected as these people do not mingle with us quite friendly.

Such a mild case of nervousness and a tinge of stage fright was revealed through the cold hands of my dad to this nun. Though my dad did not have stage fear during the time, but, as I said, it was mild.

Medically, cold hands can be understood in this way. The body triggers a fight or flee situation response. This response is usually triggered when we face a predator or a danger about to attack. Adrenaline is generated and the heart draws away blood from the organ of the body most vulnerable or in the line of attack. Needless to say, here, it is the hand. Hence, the hand becomes cooler.

This could be noticed in the people who are dead. There is no blood in their body. Hence it is very cold.

In the above situation of a mild case of stage fright in my dad, the predator is unseen. The reason being this, the mind is confused where the predator is and the body is still preparing to face attack from the predator. This causes the nervousness mixed with fear.

Rough palm

When shaking hands if the person's palms are found to have a hard/rough texture, it can mean a lot of things. To be precise, rough texture of palm of the hand can indicate the person is doing a lot of hard labour or physical work.

Such physical work can mean a person who is a mechanic; working in a machining tools division; handling hard metal parts; foundry; forging or even digging and other construction work like bar-bending. One can only speculate.

I had a friend since school days. He had mildly rough hands as I can remember since we played during the school and after hours. The person had quite a steely frame and was a determined, street-smart individual brought up in a tough environment and the hard way. Gradually, he finished his pre-university degree and sought jobs to make a living.

I met him after a long time and quite a time since he joined a job in the city, I could sense while shaking hands that his palms were very rough. Upon asking, he surmised that since he was working in the tools division and being a mechanical engineer by profession, it was obvious.

He was handling and adept at fabrication of steel products. It also gave an impression of being tough on the outside- a very important trait of 'manliness' and a seasoned individual, I suppose. The person was being bred tough.

As an afterthought, I had very soft hands since my school days. My friends used to ask me all the time that how come I have got very soft hands. It is true that I am not used to hard physical labour even now. But I am mentally very strong and have been through challenging or difficult situations in my lifetime.

To put things into perspective, having rough palms does not mean that the person is brought up the hard way or seen many difficult situations in life. But it just implies that they have been through hard physical labour. To be strong mentally and psychologically is totally a different aspect. One should not be misled. This nonverbal cue can be superficial and one needs to dig deeper.

Doctors too have very rough palms because of constantly needing to disinfect their hands with soap or alcohol-laced sanitizers to ward off the possibility of contracting germs. This is because they deal all the time with diseases and germs frequently exposed to the risk. Even the surgeries they conduct can be botched up if they do not disinfect themselves and keep the environment sterile. It is a known fact.

Misleading cues

Rough palms can also be found in people during the winter season. These are called chapped winter hands caused by wild winds, damp cold rain or snow and dry indoor heat. The cold, wet weather can take away the protective barrier posed by the skin to defend itself.

The best way to avoid being misled by such chapped hands into believing a physically hard bred personality is look to the palm of the person. There will be white, scaly formation on the skin.

Another quite misleading cue could be that the person is a germaphobe and is used to washing his hands and disinfecting them all the time, causing his palms to become rough. As noted, there are a myriad of other possibilities and skin conditions too like eczema or psoriasis. A good amount of experience is required to judge the person's thorough bred character or other cues suggesting it.

Sweaty or greasy palm

A sweaty or greasy palm can mean that the person in question is nervous. Some people have a vomit smell on their sweat. Again, these can be because of underlying medical conditions too. But can serve as a good nonverbal cue to add to your arsenal of knowledge about the person and what is going on in his mind for further consideration of your next move.

You may have noticed people breaking into sweat and adjusting their shirt collar during some uneasy questions put forth to them. The scenario could be a difficult and unanswerable question supposed to be answered during a job interview. The interviewee can be caught in a fix not knowing what to do.

The same is true with the palm breaking into sweat during a handshake. The handshake can be extended to the person in question while taking a leave from him and just a moment after asking the uncomfortable question. Some people may hide such a truth in words, but not in the handshake.

Misleading cues

Again, a sweaty palm could not suggest this in every other person. Some people may sweat normally all the time. I have a cousin who sweats all the time and his palms are greasy for most part of the day. He even covers himself in thick fleece blankets during the summer season and loves to be drenched in sweat. One should discern among such cues.

A firm handshake

This is an obvious notion everyone is familiar with. A firm handshake means the person is very confident and extroverted. Nowadays, everyone wants to put people into believing that they possess these qualities and give a firm handshake. But if done unawares, this suggests the true nature of a person. It depends upon how you can extract this information through the person unawares.

Women who have firmer handshakes too do not have a shy or introverted behaviour.

Also, people who have a very firm handshake can mean they are wanting to dominate and one needs to keep an eye out on them to be sure a gentle relationship or conversation is ensued.

Conclusion

A handshake is the most hyped form of nonverbal cues in the western society. Though there are many documented ways to know what is running in a person's mind or their intent through it, many don't know the full potential of a handshake to unearth the same. A careful observation of the different ways to unravel and what to look for can do wonders to the way people live and understand others around.

Although, no such nonverbal cues exist to give a full understanding of the state of an individual's mind, many traits can come to light that are beneficial to forge a relationship or gauge an intent or fears existing or liveliness or brought-up or the mettle that he possesses.

There are still other body language or non-verbal cues to look for in the coming chapters. These we will discuss in detail.

References

www.calmclinic.com/anxiety/symptoms/cold-hands

www.today.com/health/chapped-winter-hands-it-dry-skin-or-something-else-t208822

www.apa.org/news/press/releases/2000/07/hand-shake

Sniffle

The meaning of sniffle can be understood by someone who has caught a cold and has a runny nose anytime in his life. A sniffle is the reaction you produce when the nose leaks or runs with a watery substance i.e., mucus or snot. You try to contain in it in the nose by sniffing it in or breathing hard through your nostrils. This is done every time the nose runs.

Now that the meaning of sniffle is laid out bare, an important body language or nonverbal cue can be understood that openly shows whether a person is telling lies; guilty or cheating.

Cheating is rampant everywhere in any society, community or locality. It knows no barrier of race, caste, creed, religion, background or anything. Everyone wants to make quick money by bypassing the natural law of earning through hard work wherein the ground was cursed at the creation and wouldn't give out fruits and food without tilling.

This kind of vice is found while we travel; commute; do business; buy something; run errands; ask questions and get misleading answers; pay for anything and the seller demands excess; and the like. Cab drivers may cheat us with the fare or merchants with the price or malicious people with an aim to gain profits for themselves can do this.

There is a way to steer clear from all of this and remain safe without getting into a loss. The sign to look out for in such malicious and damnable individuals is a sniffle. It betrays the intention of the person in question and a good observer can remain safe.

The moment a person is lying or cheating, there comes a sniffle in their body language. There are many instances in my life wherein I was privy to this great truth. I will share one by one.

Instance 1

Once I was asked by my mother to buy some leafy vegetables to cook for dinner while I was going for my evening walk quite a few years ago.

As I was searching for a suitable hawker who was selling these bunch of spinach on the roadside, I found one person in the twilight.

He was a young man in his late teens. Many people were buying the leafy vegetables from him- spinach, dill, fenugreek leaves and what not. This man sold to a middle-aged lady a bunch of spinach or dill—I suppose—and was trying to make quick money by selling it to me at a higher price.

The price for it—at the time—was normally ₹10 for a regular size of bunch. And this was only speculative as some days the price can go up by ₹5 or ₹10 or so, above the normal.

When I enquired the price directly to him, he quoted ₹15. This was more than ₹5 the normal price for a bunch of spinach mentioned before. So, when I asked him the price, the person after a few moments gave out a sniffle. This, he did, though he was not suffering from cold or a runny nose.

The sniffle coming out from a healthy individual as him who is not suffering from cold or an allergic reaction, is a clear indication that the hawker was guilty and was cheating me with an exaggerated price way above normal for a bunch of spinach in the area.

I backtracked from buying the bunch from him and sternly asked for the normal ongoing price of ₹10. He did not budge and—as is the custom in our part of the country to walk away from the place and the sellers call us back for the asked price—I walked away. He called me back and I bought it for the normal price- a good two fresh bunch of spinach. Being done for the day, completed my daily routine of walk amidst nature and reached home.

Instance 2

We constructed our house some ten years ago. The finishing work was under progress. There was a need for a granite slab for the kitchen counter-top. My brother and me ventured out to look for a very good granite slab provider in our locality. The shop which instantly came to my mind was a merchant who was nearby and owned quite a number of varieties of granite having a huge area where he stacked them up.

We went there, zeroed in on a good granite slab and stood in a queue to buy it for use in the construction of our new house. A person had come to buy a different variety of slab and was acting smart. I noticed that he got cheated without his knowledge and went about his routine for the day.

Next was our turn. My brother and I had to bargain like the other person who left before us for the granite slab, we were about to buy. The man at the counter was dressed very well and, I think, had a full two sachet of pan masala stocked in his mouth. He was spewing crimson-coloured saliva from his mouth.

The person was armed with a calculator and was about to quote a price to us for the granite stone we decided to buy. He made some calculations with it involving some percentage it would cost him and other profit-loss equations. Later, he blurted out a price and we did not know what was the right price for the granite in that area for the time.

He sniffled and touched his nose a few times while quoting the price for the slab. I could clearly see that he was cheating and his guilt shown in this nonverbal cue. Needless to say, I revealed to my brother that the person was exaggerating the price.

My brother replied that we could do nothing and the person was taking advantage of the situation. The situation being that this was the only person in our whole area who had such stones and buying it from other places—which are quite far—could incur transportation charges for it. This being, the slab is very heavy.

So, we returned home settling for the price and the vendor. Our work was done.

Instance 3

This incident is during my early adolescent years. I had dropped out from an engineering college for quite a time—that doesn't matter now as my career path has changed—and there was pressure at home to look for a job and earn a decent pay. Though I was not ready for this kind of 'livelihood' as the kind of job being offered was quite a personal put off for me.

The reason for this could be that I don't have a passion for such desk jobs like cashier or teller or insurance company field executive or even data entry operator. Another reason could be that I had to land a job that requires skills that I possess; the pay scale was never the bone of contention for me.

In fact, there were a number of resumé prepared by me and almost frequent interviews that I gave to different prospective employers. These were done with formal attire—as is the norm—with my recently graduated cousins from the native who lived in the city and were looking for a good lifestyle through landing jobs in MNCs.

There was one such incident wherein my dad had opted for a life insurance policy in a pleasant insurance group. The insurance agent of this private firm—which was an MNC—had grown close enough to him to seek an employment offer for me from his bosses.

The job was that of a tele caller who would all the time call different phone numbers to get them insured in the company. There was just a phone on the desk and this cold calling job was offered to me. There were very high expectations from me that I was an engineering student and a good fit for the role; the manager was impressed.

Though they offered good money and perks, I was unimpressed because of the many reasons listed above.

Before I had visited this office, they had called me over the phone to schedule an interview. As I said, the idea of working there was not on my mind. I had switched off my smartphone just to avoid this whole interview thing. I hoped to somehow escape from this situation and at the same time avoid unpleasant talks about career or confrontations regarding the 'what do you want to do in life?' kind of questions from people known to me.

I did not think that this whole idea of switching off my smartphone would bring some kind of turbulence in the office and also for the insurance agent my dad was close to.

When I visited the office of this MNC, there was a good amount of bustling workplace activity everywhere around. And I passed by this insurance agent who wanted to do a 'good thing' in my life giving me the employment opportunity.

As I was moving around in the office, this person was sniffling and touching his nose a few times. I did not understand as to why he was doing it. But it stayed in my mind for quite a number of years- the whole picture of him doing it.

Later I found out that he had trapped my dad by selling an insurance policy that was very expensive and not beneficial in the long run. My dad is not used to read the long terms and conditions stated in such documents. He took it for the agent's word that it was a good policy for him.

My dad had to continue this life insurance policy for a very long time paying huge premiums and the term ended many years later.

This fiasco brought to light many things to me: one of them was the sniffling and touching of the nose this insurance agent was doing. Clearly, he was guilty and the nonverbal cue of sniffling with touching of the nose revealed this. A good observer can notice this.

Instance 4

There are many instances of people close to me like cousins sniffling while sharing certain rumours about other relatives. I catch them then and there as telling lies or just rumour mongering.

Misleading cues

Though it is true that when people sniffle, they are telling lies or guilty or cheating, it is nonetheless also true that they do not sniffle every time they do this. There are many instances in my life wherein no one sniffled or touched their nose while they were up to something like such malicious behaviour.

One can complement this nonverbal cue with asking many other related questions to know if people are lying. To be precise, if someone tells you that a known person had finished his PhD, more questions can be put forth to him.

Questions like, 'Which was the university he earned that degree from?' and 'Who was his instructor?' When such questions are brought forth the person will have no answers in his kitty and may fumble or bluntly give inane answers.

Comparing those answers elsewhere with the person's close confidante reveals the true colours of the one who said that. If these don't match with the former person's answers, the main question was a lie. To arrive at this many questions should be asked and their answers collected.

Also, there are people who keep touching their noses and sniffling all the time. This does not mean that they are telling lies or cheating or guilty. It just means that it is their habit and other ways can be tried with them like the former one. There are many such people.

One of my immediate neighbours is a leader of some activity or workshop in the Church. During one of the meetings to discuss an activity for the Church's cleaning and decoration, he was addressing all the inductees regarding the tasks each one of them has to undertake.

He used to sniffle and touch his nose all the time even though there was nothing that could point to being guilty or cheating or lying. This is his habit while he addresses people or during public speaking. Again, not to be confused with the intentions revealing sniffling we are talking about here.

Moreover, people with a slight cold and have a runny nose should not be confused as guilty of these vices. There are many such people around and one could mistake them easily as doing such. There should be some discretion.

Conclusion

Being adept with the art of identifying such malicious people through sniffling can benefit a lot in our everyday activity. Most importantly, one can make wise decisions while availing a service as to whether it is beneficial or hurting our pockets. The day-to-day activity as such mentioned herein in the instances like buying; one-time investment like constructing a house; using any service like carpentry for building house furniture or interior decoration services cannot become burdensome or too much heavy on the pockets through this nonverbal cue.

Any good observer can remain safe and steer away from people with malicious intent while deciding to go ahead with the person's services or not. No one can cheat a wise person. One has to rely on this basic knowledge and the possibilities are limitless. There is more to come in the pages to follow.

Playing With The Feet

There is yet another nonverbal cue wherein a person's mental disposition can be discerned as to whether he is justifying himself. This justifying can also be a sign that he was into a fight with somebody moments before. Moments in the sense some seconds ago.

The sign to look out for is that the person plays with his feet as drawing something on the ground. It need not necessarily mean drawing but playing with the mud or stones too while he is standing after the tiff or quarrel.

Also, this nonverbal cue from the person could not be done only on the muddy ground but anywhere on the floor where he is standing. But the action should be like he is playing with the mud or moving stones and gravel with his feet.

More so, this cue can also mean that the person exhibiting it has a change of mind or repented from the opinion he had prior to the truth unfolding in front of his eyes. The thought is intimidating to him and he wants to change his stance on the matter.

There are a few instances in my life wherein I observed this nonverbal cue in people.

Instance 1

I was working in a startup with the position of a Content Writer. It was a consulting firm and later I was moved to a software sister concern. There was a person who was working with me assisting the firm in the accounting department.

He was a middle-aged man, quite experienced in the profession and earning well for his position. Some days passed and there was turmoil in his extended family life. His sister ran into some problem head on and this was nagging him all the time. I could see it in his behaviour at office.

As it was severely affecting his work life, he resorted to the habit of drinking alcohol to alleviate it. Gradually, the alcohol intake increased and his breath was smelling of it. He used to come to office drunk.

Also, there was no punctuality wherein he would drop in to office middle of the day. My employer became aware of it and asked him regarding the downward spiraling work ethic. To all our—and his colleagues'—surprise he revealed to the boss that he is drinking lately and there is a problem in his extended family. He was plain.

The boss called him to the board room and a confrontation ensued. There was a lot of loud talk for a few minutes and he sent him home. Me and my fellow colleagues couldn't overhear the conversation.

After the confrontation, my boss returned to the working area and we could see him standing. He was playing with his feet just as I mentioned above. Needless to say, he was justifying himself regarding the decision he had taken to fire the senior accountant from his job. This was right after the confrontation and heated exchange.

This act of justifying is understood as having a job is very helpful and precious for everyone. A family and its expenses depend on it. It is dear for anyone. So, the boss was justifying himself for a few minutes with this nonverbal cue and he left home after a while.

Instance 2

Years ago, a news story ran on a televised media channel. It was regarding a well-known television personality about how he was involved in a life-threatening motor accident with another famous personality. They were airing videos and pictures of this television personality moments after the high-profile accident in which there was no loss of life but grave damage to the vehicles.

As they were telecasting these videos of the man and his wife being bruised, the whole blame of the accident was put on the driver of the person. It was also aired that the personality was not driving the car in which the accident occurred, but the chauffeur was.

The visuals of the chauffeur were aired too continuously all the time. But I could make out that the television personality was telling lies and he, himself, was involved in the accident and driving the car. I, even, was sure that this person put the blame on the driver forcefully and blatantly.

The reason for this assertion by me was that the driver exhibited the nonverbal cue of playing with his feet on all the visuals displayed on the television screen. He was looking down with his arms tied around his back and continuously playing with his feet as if searching or drawing something in the gravel or dirt or soil.

Though this person was forced into admitting that he was on the wheels of the car during the time of the accident, there was no resistance from him. He willfully admitted it out of his own volition.

The whole behind-the-scenes scenario to unfold before us is that a strong one-sided verbal attack ensued on the driver and he was intimidated, having no option to say otherwise. He may have been forced into believing that his job was threatened or it was so.

He was continuously justifying during the nonverbal cue exhibition about the possibilities or permutations and combinations of what he could have done to avoid getting into the eyes of this irate television personality. And also, how he could have escaped out of this situation in a better way than how it unfurled.

The blatant lie from the television personality regarding the veracity of the claim of who was on the wheels of the car during the crash was exposed with this nonverbal cue. A very handy one, indeed! I got to know the mind of the television personality and the kind of situation he puts his employees in. His whole mindset in the situation was laid bare before me.

Truly, rich people rule the roost in our society.

Instance 3

Recently, an incident unfolded that lends weight to this cue developing visually. I was watching television passively—as I always do and not actively—and there ran a story in the news about a country achieving a rare and immense feat in astronomy.

The leader of the country was addressing some form of assembly of delegates and while he announced the feat being achieved live on the screen, a member or a delegate exhibited this nonverbal cue.

This he did because he had thought that the country which achieved this feat was not developed technologically enough to do so. But with the event unfolding right in front of his eyes, he changed his stance.

Though this person was not seated with his lower torso visible enough to judge about this nonverbal cue, still I managed to perceive that he was exhibiting it. And to say the least, the feat achieved by this country was worth remembering.

Misleading cue

Many people play with their feet in this way during a leisurely time too- when at liberty with their friends. This should not be confused with the original nonverbal cue to know when a person has come clean out of a tiff.

Conclusion

The emotion behind this nonverbal cue of playing with the feet is pure and its raw potential can only be imagined. Imagine if a person is exhibiting this nonverbal cue and you are to discuss a prospect of business with him. His mind is not calm and may be wandering. And this is not the right time to talk sense with him like peaceful discussions on philosophy.

But it should be noted that sometimes the tiff may be very severe and the severity cannot be measured with this nonverbal cue. One should let the justifying thoughts sink in with time.

As noted in the Instance 1, my employer went home to let time heal his emotions that had come out of this fiasco with the accountant. Time heals almost everything.

The Perfectionist Touch

This nonverbal cue reveals that the person who does it is insecure superficially and being persecuted about his credentials of capability, it may totally make sense that he is highly capable- not to say the least. Also, it is a false insecurity. A clearer picture may emerge in the instances that follow. But first, more about the action in the nonverbal cue.

The perfectionist touch, here, is when a person touches the items available on his desk or vanity bag or close vicinity as if to arrange them in an order or structure or stack. These items may be newspapers, files, documents, magazines under the paperweight. Sometimes, the touch could be just a tap or dab on the vanity bag or anything.

There are many instances in my life where I observed this nonverbal cue at work in everyday people.

Instance 1

I have the habit of attending daily mass at our local parish church. On one of the days, I was doing the same. There had come a visiting priest from a nearby college run by priests of a particular congregation. The college was a few miles away.

As the priest began celebrating mass, he reached the stage of giving a sermon midway through it. He was describing about the importance of education and his life journey that led him to be a priest with a calling.

The priest was known to my brother who heard many of his lectures during college days. And he was known to have won many laurels from his alma mater and his university. There were a few gold medals credited to him from these institutions.

During the sermon, when preaching about the importance of education, he revealed the gold medal won by him in different subjects. The state ranks he had won were a few of them and he stated them in quite a modest manner.

I was watching him the whole time when he spoke passionately about the medals he had won. Quite interestingly, he exhibited the perfectionist touch nonverbal cue and touched the few sheets of paper—maybe that had the important points of the sermon written in it so that he can elaborate—in front of him two or three times.

The lessons to be drawn from this is that—as stated at the beginning of the chapter—the priest was highly capable in the academic field he was speaking about. Having won many laurels from his alma mater, the nonverbal cue suggested just the same about him. It can gauge the capability of anybody.

Instance 2

I was working in a consulting firm a few years back and we were a modest five to six employees at the branch in our city. There was a woman employee working with us. She was quite in her late 40's, I suppose. The woman was from a well-to-do family and her husband was known for his high-profile contacts.

As most of the workforce was relatives and friends of the founders and directors, we were all casually chatting. The chat was about high paying jobs some people had landed. As the directors were quite well-to-do, midway in the chat, she shared about the lifestyle at her home.

While doing so, she gave the perfectionist touch to her vanity bag that was lying on the desk. She had her bag all readied up as it was time for her to leave after working half day. This act of hers made sure to me that she was indeed well-off and a large part of her family's affluent lifestyle was evident in her day-to-day banter with us at the workplace.

Conclusion

This nonverbal cue is a litmus test and is very truthful of the things it reveals. I think it is more truthful than the truth serum or the polygraph test. It has many applications wherein the truth is revealed as to whether people are what they speak. And if they are what they speak—if exhibiting this nonverbal cue of the perfectionist touch—they are very good at it.

Quite notably, this nonverbal cue can signify that the person in question is not to be messed with- the last person to quarrel with.

The Horizon Search

As the name suggests, this nonverbal cue manifests itself in a person as if he is searching for something nearby. It may be searching something on the monitor at the workplace or out of the nearby window or in the shop. To a person who is noticing this nonverbal cue the searching would seem pointless as there is nothing noteworthy or making sense to find.

Also, this futile searching action with the whole body involved- sometimes standing or at other times in the sitting position—wherever the person is seated—may also seem a normal work routine like looking at the smartphone for recent notifications or even looking to the wall clock as to what time it is telling.

In all essence, this nonverbal cue is exhibited when a person is hurt at the taunt or question or anything posed to him during the conversation. This hurt may not be very painful but superficial. It can have applications in bargaining the right price for the commodity or item you are about to purchase, as you may notice it in the real instances in my life where I witnessed them. Here, they follow one by one.

Instance 1

I was at home during an afternoon and was doing nothing sort of worth telling, whiling away time. This was during my job searching days. Out of the blue, there appeared a relative of ours who lived some miles away from our home in the city and very rarely visited us. She was quite close to my mother since her younger days and shared a seemingly alleged good bond with her.

Being the wily and crafty lady that she is, upon entering she passed a taunt and it was directed towards me. She is still known to be a prominent gossip monger in our native, ganging up together with the other known ones from her group to discuss ongoing affairs in the whole neighbourhood and city.

Coming to the point, the taunt directed towards me was a question regarding me not finding a job anywhere in the city since I was in the job searching age of my life. This age is just a number and adds fuels to the rumour mills in the neighbourhood.

Needless to say, this gossip was very interesting and widespread during that time and she had to carry the news about it to her fellow gossip mongers who asked about it. Practically, there is no age or physical condition to land a high-status or well-respected job anywhere. Believe me.

Just when the lady passed the taunt as to your son does nothing at all to my mother, I exhibited this nonverbal cue. The way I exhibited it stuck with me for a long time until I understood about it deeply.

I just replied to her that I am searching for a suitable job for myself and standing up from the chair on which I was seated, looked outside our main door as if searching for someone there. My whole body was involved in this nonverbal cue and I was hurt because of this wily lady's taunt.

My mother, fed her some interesting gossip which was all lies and sent her away so that she may know later as to who are the people this news reaches too. Those were interesting days. As I may say, 'The process is punishing, but the thought is beautiful'. These days have stuck with me in memories.

Instance 2

There comes another instance to my mind wherein this nonverbal cue was exhibited before my eyes. Once I visited a relative of mine to ask something about a bug in the software of my recently bought laptop as the person was a software engineer and knew many things about computers.

Me, my cousin who took me there and the software engineer were talking about different topics. Then the conversation took a different route and moved towards the job or workplace issues in the person's office. This is always the case as my cousin is used to speak about workplace matters all the time with anybody he meets.

The moment my cousin asked the engineer about his profile at work and the kind of workplace atmosphere, he exhibited this nonverbal cue. The manner in which he did it was interesting: he was working on the computer on his desk at home and while talking, he looked at the monitor narrowing down his eyes as if he had searched something. Then he returned to normal.

As a matter of fact, there was nothing noteworthy to look at the monitor, but he did it. And also, it simply implies there are two things to be noted. One was that he was visibly hurt and—from quite deep inside too—he was not employed with any company at the moment.

I understood that he was unemployed. The fact of this matter was quite revealing to me in that all of his immediate family members were lying about him landing a job and doing well in his profession all the time. Truly, nothing can be hidden from a good observer.

Instance 3

This instance is quite interesting as it is related to know about ways of effectively bargaining for a product one wants to buy from a shop.

I had the habit of moving around with my brother and sister-in-law in our car while they were running errands for themselves or just a long drive on the weekend or other leisurely activities. So, one day we were in the mood to shop for badminton racquets and reached a well-known bustling shopping center in our city.

This shopping center was packed with many sports shops. We zeroed in on one good shop and were looking at the racquets there. My brother got his eyes on a good professional racquet as he himself was a state-level badminton player.

So—as my sister-in-law is good at bargaining a price that suits us—she started doing it with the owner of the shop. She asked for a price and the shopkeeper said it is not the right price to sell his goods.

Hence, she lowered down her asking price and the person was not happy with the price too. As she is good at these things, my sister-in-law figured out the cost price of the badminton racquet on some reputed online store and stuck to the price.

This price is quite burdensome for a brick-and-mortar shop owner because the distribution model and other aspects of online stores are different. And thus, they cannot keep up with the price that they offer. So, we stuck around that price as a reference.

When we got around that price for the third asking price, the shopkeeper exhibited this nonverbal cue. He started looking at some racquet near him narrowing his eyes down as if he had searched and found something on it.

He was visibly hurt at the prospect of not getting the right price he had bought the racquet from his distributor. This is the price at which the profit for the shopkeeper was almost zero and this margin caused a concern in him.

Anyway, we bought the racquet for around this price and left the place; the price was quite a fit and worth our hard-earned money.

Misleading cues

One should not be misled by behaviour and gestures that are similar to this nonverbal cue. People may just be looking at their smartphone and not necessarily exhibiting this cue. They may do this to look for notifications or messages or the time or even looking for scorecard of sportsmen or other things as these are repetitive behaviour. One can be easily misled.

Conclusion

As depicted before, this nonverbal cue is very handy when bargaining for items sold in the marketplace. But the limitation of this cue is that the person should be visible and preferably present before our eyes to gauge his mindset through it.

One factor to look out for in this nonverbal cue is that the person narrows his eyes down considerably and looks tense while exhibiting it. This is obvious as he is hurt in his heart. If this factor is check boxed, the horizon search is definitely at work in the person's gesture and the price for effectively bargaining with the vendor can be fixed. It never lies as it comes from the heart.

Anger-Exhibiting Cue

This cue is exhibited when a person is angry- maybe greatly, and also is restless. This nonverbal cue is defined by the person shaking or moving his feet horizontally when in seated position. He may do it in spells and intervals or continuously. As the person thinks about what offended him, he keeps doing the action or nonverbal cue.

Benefits

When a person exhibits this nonverbal cue, it is wise to let the person calm down from his anger. Or in other words, one should wait until this person stops shaking his legs in this manner completely—not also in intervals or spells—to ask favour or learn something from him. As it can be derived, he won't help you until his anger has ceased.

Instance

I was privy to one such incident and would note this nonverbal cue in my higher management staff who was working with me around my cubicle. As this was a startup, higher management officials would work with us on the same floor and without cabins.

The person was offended by me for some silly thing because he can get irate easily. He was shaking his legs vigorously and I understood the action from me hit him the most at his heart. The reason for his anger was that he wanted some help from me regarding formatting a personal letter; I refused and made some face without knowing he was looking right into me.

His anger slowly subsided as I saw it in this nonverbal cue wherein the shaking of the leg vigorously slowly subsided into intervals and later, completely stopped. Then I approached him for some help. We asked help from him for everything as he was a consultant with more than five to six decades of experience in managing and execution of different projects- a CEO level officer.

Misleading cues

Though this cue may prove to be a sneak peek into a person's mind whether he is angry or not, it can be quite confusing. This is because many people have the habit of shaking their legs in this manner—horizontally—when they are idle or at leisure. It is like a pastime for them.

To avoid this confusion, one needs to be adept or experienced enough to distinguish between these two situations. One of these ways to distinguish is the speed or the vigour with which this shaking is done. If there is too much vigour involved, it definitely means the person is quite angry with the recent statement made by someone. Better to allow him to calm down.

Conclusion

This cue is quite a revelation in a person's mind. But sometimes the legs of a person are out of the line of sight. The best way to avoid this is to have a furniture set up wherein these are easily visible. One should draw experience from visits to a psychologist or a related specialty medical professional.

Even if this nonverbal cue is hidden out of sight from the observer, an experienced one can distinguish whether the anger emotion is involved or not. The reason being some shakiness in the upper torso too. Quite understandably.

Fear-Exhibiting Cue

This cue is another form of the recently discussed one. While exhibiting this cue, people shake their legs in an up and down or vertical fashion. The person who is the subject of this cue is fearing for something that is intimidating or quite out of his bounds that may happen to him.

Sometimes, the truth may come out to the observer as to what this person is fearing right in the conversation. Else, the truth may be hidden from the person who notices this nonverbal cue in the subject.

There are numerous instances in my life wherein I was left with a deep insight into a person's character through this nonverbal cue. Some of them follow below.

Instance 1

I was once admitted in a hospital. Being an inpatient, a medical professional evaluated me during the first few days of my stay there. He asked many questions. Later, through the course of these questions, he came directly to the cause for the symptoms I exhibited; he bluntly revealed his diagnosis possibly to know the nonverbal cue or reaction I was giving out.

As the diagnosis was of quite a debilitating illness, I exhibited this nonverbal cue. There was fear in my mind and the medical practitioner saw my legs through the table. He asked me whether I was scared. Needless to record my response, he stood up and went away revealing it to his senior doctors.

Instance 2

There comes to mind a movie wherein a person who bombed a school is interrogated by an investigative agency official. The subject was seated in an interrogation setup with a table and a chair that are essential to record such nonverbal cues. Then he was asked about the whole process as to how he managed to do it.

Midway through the conversation, the subject was asked by the agent whether he was scared. This was when the bomber shaking his legs somewhat vigorously up and down in a vertical fashion. The mind of this criminal was laid bare before him.

Instance 3

Once after quite a few years of being employed as a Content Writer, I was attending mass at my parish church. This was the same church and parish to which my cousins and their family belonged but now I have moved to a different locality altogether; hence, a different church and parish.

My cousin with his family too was attending mass in the church on a Sunday. But he—as was his usual custom—was attending the mass outside in the premises of the church. The mass ended and after the recession hymn, I was making my way out of the church with my family.

I met this cousin of mine and his family. Without hesitation, I asked him whether he was hearing mass from outside the church. He was scared of what to answer quite understandably because I had a moral authority and some social status as of then.

Just when I asked, he exhibited this nonverbal cue. It should be noted that he was in the standing position and his legs were shaking front and back quite vigorously. Visibly as noticed by an observer i.e., me, he feared a dip in his likeability among the extended family of our cousins.

Then he replied with some vague answer, we extended a handshake and other pleasantries setting on our way home.

Instance 4

There was also an incident that I can recall through which I got familiar with this nonverbal cue. I was returning home from my office commuting by a bus after a day's work in the evening. As I got a seat in the bus, there was a fellow traveler. He was on his journey may be to run some errands.

I could notice his legs shaking up and down while he was in the seated position. This is to mean that the commuter was fearing thinking about how to go about his journey. Quite understandably, about how to find the proper address or catch the required train plying to this address or the manner in which he will reach the destination.

These anxious moments set off this nonverbal cue in him of fear. He did this shaking of the legs in intervals and spells. This is to mean that he was thinking in between about this yoke of anxiety on him in intervals and rested in-between them.

Conclusion

This nonverbal cue is quite helpful in determining a person's state of mind and one can pacify him though encouragement or kind words. Another aspect of this cue is that if the subject exhibits it all the time in different parts of the day at different intervals, he is a person who worries a lot.

My mother does this regularly and worries a lot about everything. I suspect the worries are mostly about her children and their everyday whereabouts or safety/well-being; her legs are set in motion always.

This is not a handicap as such people are very productive and efficient at everything they undertake, nonetheless. Another great peek into the mind.

The Smartness-Exhibiting Cue

This nonverbal cue suggests that the person exhibiting it is thinking he made a smart move or made a brilliant statement in his conversation. To talk into detail, this person shows on the face as eating something with his mouth, but, in fact, he is not. He is just doing the action of eating something.

I can enumerate many incidents in my life where this nonverbal cue was exhibited.

Instance 1

Our family has just moved from a distant place to the city. As these were very early days in the city, there were many things we were in the dark about the way of life here or how people lived. A salesman reached our rented house and began to talk to us so that he can sell the products he was carrying. We, as a family, could not find on ways how to politely reject his sales pitch.

Hence, we turned to my younger brother as he was quite street-smart since his younger days and had traveled a lot for his state and national sports championship events.

After answering and dealing with the salesman, my brother exhibited this nonverbal cue by as if chewing/eating something with his mouth, but there was nothing to chew/eat. Needless to say, he thought it was a smart move and he did well.

Instance 2

In another instance, I was walking in the evening—as was my daily routine during those days—and I entered a vegetable store to buy some vegetables because my mother had asked me to. As I was entering the store, a person had just paid his bill for the vegetables he had bought at the counter and the vendor was exhibiting this nonverbal cue.

He thought that he was smart in dealing with this previous customer and next was my turn.

Misleading cue

One thing to be noted is that there are some quite elderly people who exhibit such actions as if this cue is given out. This is done by them because of loss of teeth. But they are actually not exhibiting this cue as they tend to do this and it is natural because of their advanced years. And this part of their behaviour is to be overlooked as not fitting into being smart.

Conclusion

To my thought, it appeared that in the second instance just shared, I should not ask him some inane question like how was his day or how is life. This is because I would have got a retort back like days are always fine or 'what can happen to life?'

People who just have exhibited this nonverbal cue think that they are smart and give such quite rude replies or show some attitude ignoring the asker or the one who is conversing with them. It is better to avoid talking to them or asking questions for a while until they come back to their own old selves.

Also, it is to be noted that they think they are smart, but it need not be true. There are plenty of other instances to share. But I think these are enough to learn.

Callousness-Exhibiting Cue

A person exhibiting this cue is acting or talking in a callous manner. The nonverbal cue to look out for in this emotion is when on a video call over the smartphone, the person shows his teeth as if checking how his teeth look or check for something stuck in his teeth. Also, it may seem that—in the video call—the subject is checking or pinching his pimples or making some faces. All of this depends on the person.

Since a few years, I was always wondering what this nonverbal cue meant as I would see myself too doing this kind of action when I was talking with someone over the phone. I received inspiration about this just while writing this book as in the first instance that follows regarding my brother.

A brief description follows.

Instance

We, as a family, have an instant messaging platform group and my brother—who lives abroad—calls often in the group and we talk a lot. During one of such video calls, my brother and we siblings were all talking with each other with harmless teasing.

One of such teasing sessions went awfully wrong. He is known for such things and the results could be that I am not on talking terms with him a few hours after this episode.

The instance was that he teased my sister with a few hurtful comments regarding her life. Obviously, she did not take it in a good way and blocked us all from the group. She was visibly upset with him mainly.

Later, while talking about it, he exhibited this nonverbal cue. He does this often, making faces or showing his teeth or checking for pimples on his face in the phone camera.

Conclusion

This nonverbal cue does not mean that the person is a totally callous person. He may be a mild one. Take the instance of my brother, though he is callous sometimes, the case is mild as he won't get into fights or malice. We all at home are meek as such. But nonetheless a great nonverbal cue to watch in a person.

Anxiety Exhibiting Cue

This is a cue wherein the person concerned shakes his legs just like the anger-exhibiting cue. But this shaking of the legs horizontally or sideways is not in a very animated way and rather in a calm way. So, this cannot be confused with the anger-exhibiting cue.

Another interesting fact about this cue is that it can be witnessed in obvious places and there is no reward for guessing that. When such a feeling like anxiety comes to mind, the places that crop up are public transportation system passenger terminals, waiting lobby outside doctors' clinic, students' examination halls and more. In clear terms, waiting and fears about future can spring up anxiety and hence, this cue.

If one observes a passenger or ICU patient's attender, there is ample evidence of this nonverbal cue.

Conclusion

The people who exhibit this cue are quite tense and the gravity of this tension depends on what the scenario or situation the individual is in. Talking to them won't yield results and questions put forth to them won't fetch right answers. Also, they won't be in a cheerful mood and cracking jokes with them is not a good idea. It fits best to leave them waiting in silence.

The end result is that it pays to be smart and one who is wise can act likewise in a calculated manner.

Epilogue

Though many books are written on this subject of nonverbal cues revealing the complex minds of us humans, each of these are totally different. They deal with different kind of nonverbal cues and are not similar to each other. But reveal the same major complexity of human minds in the written work they disseminate.

Apart from these nonverbal cues, there are many others too found in people. Another body language trait I would like to talk about lastly, is fumbling during a conversation.

My prospective employer was avoiding the question of giving me an offer letter for the requirement of a job as there was no concrete development in the contract being awarded to him by his client. Because of this and a host of other reasons like the retainer not being released to him as things are slow in this time of global slowdown and the after math of the pandemic outbreak around the world and such, these things persisted.

So, I asked him about this prospect of handing over the offer letter to me and the joining date to the newly started company. As I was speaking to him over the phone, I could not rely on the nonverbal cues because of him being at a very distant place and every communication could be over a voice call through the internet.

When I posed him the question, he fumbled with his words and gave me a general not-so-obvious date. Also, he revealed to me a few developments regarding the contract being awarded, the talks going on in the management and such.

Needless to say, he was not sure about my joining date in his company. But he wanted me in the company. Hence, he revealed the developments regarding the same. The fumbling revealed the things running in his mind and I was left assured of finding an employment with him.

There are many nonverbal cues other than listed in this book. But one can draw a lot of lessons from the ones listed here and they offer a great peek into the mind of people he meets in everyday life.

As Bertrand Russell said, 'The world is full of beautiful things waiting to be unfolded by our intellect' and we just have to keep searching, learning, observing and poring over into books.

About the Author

Jude D'Souza

Jude is a Content Writer by profession with over 9 years of experience in varied forms of writing. He has written blog articles, social media posts and more for his employers including freelance gigs. His clients have described his writing style as poetic, engaging, intellectual and interesting.
Psychology has been a natural part of his life- an innate quality. He has been applying this in daily engagement with people and it has helped him immensely. Though it is used by people with complex minds, through some assistance, the attribute can be adopted.

It has been his sincere effort to disseminate and share the wisdom with the readers. They surely need to be offered some value.

He satiates his appetite for reading with books that evince curiosity, mostly biographies of great personalities, delving deeper into their lives.

He lives in Bengaluru with his immediate family and pet dog, Rover.

www.ingramcontent.com/pod-product-compliance
Lightning Source LLC
LaVergne TN
LVHW041641070526
838199LV00053B/3490